To Keith,
the bear at the end

First U.S. Edition 1992 1 2 3 4 5 6 7 8 9 10

Library of Congress Cataloging in Publication data was not available in time for publication
of this book, but can be obtained from the Library of Congress. ISBN 0-688-11232-3
ISBN 0-688-11233-1 (lib. bdg.) L.C. Number 91-53046

Polar Bear
Scare

Jill Newton

Lothrop, Lee & Shepard Books
New York

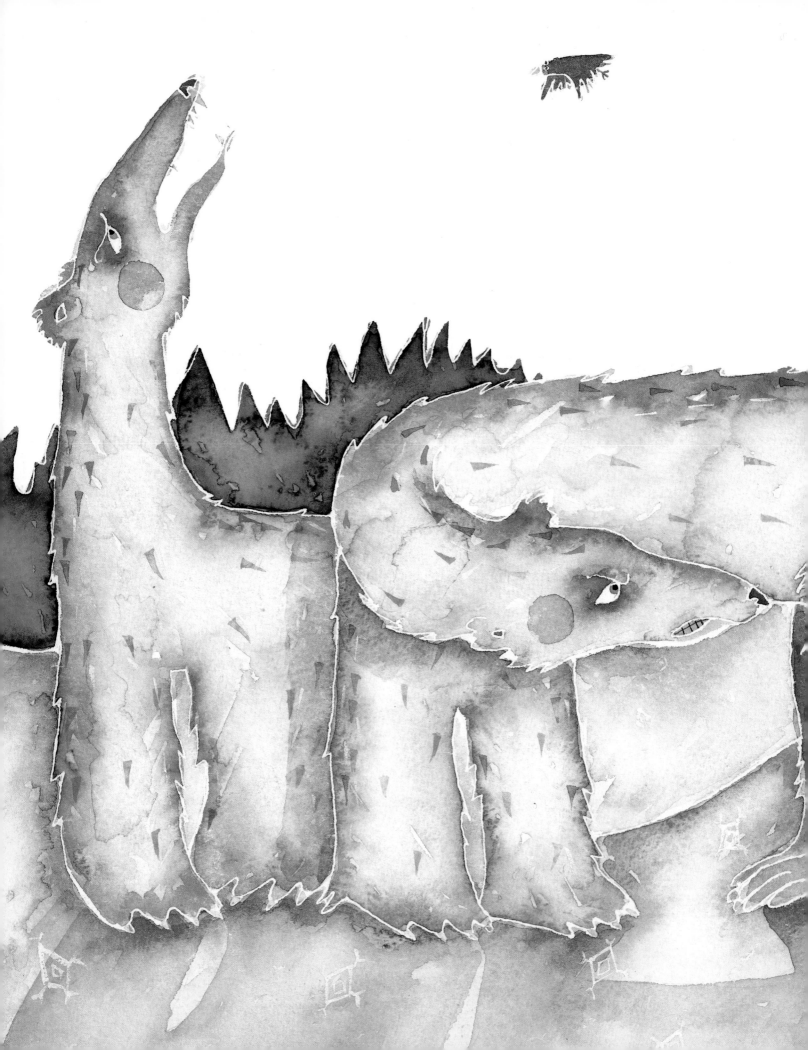

Out fishing for fish, I found three polar bears. Or, rather, they found me.

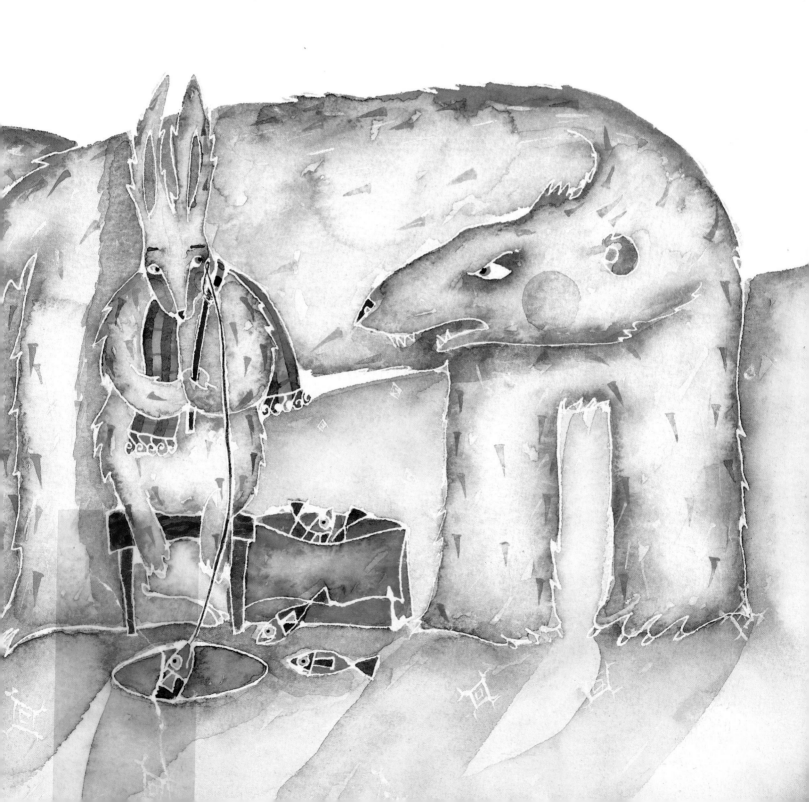

"HELP!" I shouted in my loudest voice,
but when no help came, I started to run.

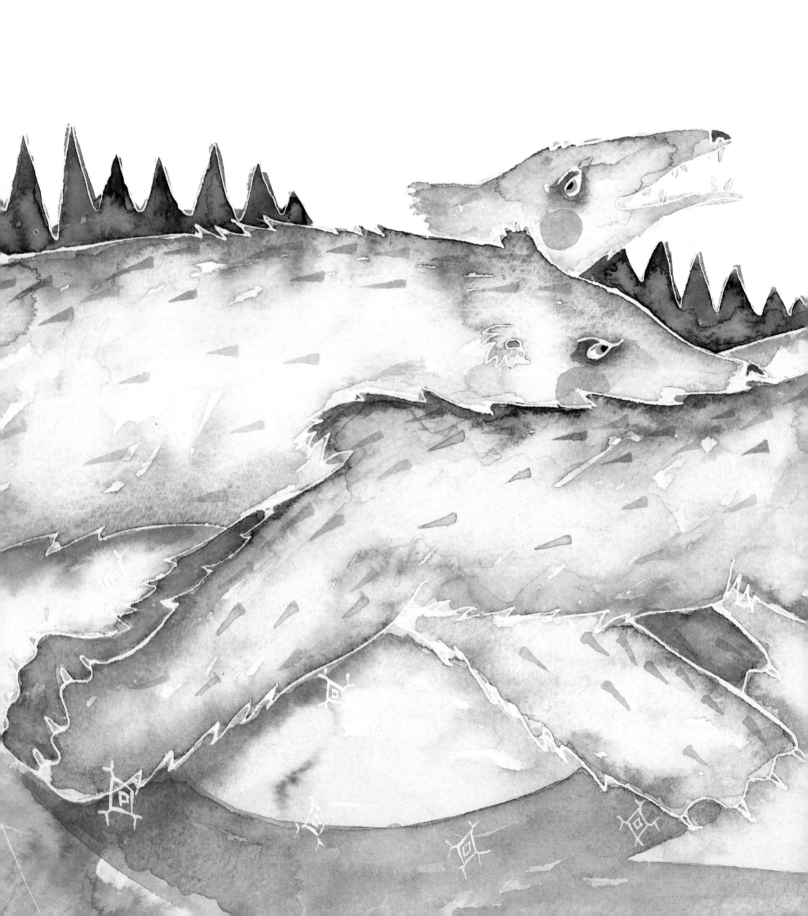

I threw some of my fish to the bears to slow them down, but they weren't interested in small fry.

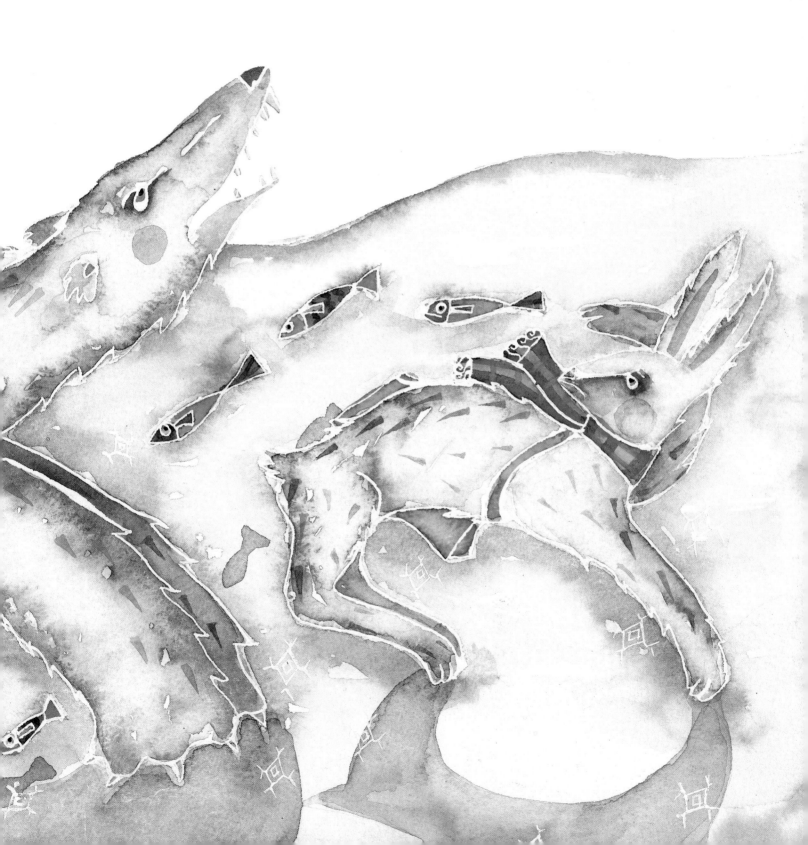

I came across a walrus and a whale and interrupted their chat. "Sorry, but I'm being chased by three polar bears," I explained as I offered them what was left of my fish. "Can you help me?"

"I'm going to the other side of the ice," said the whale. "I'll give you a lift, if you don't mind getting a bit wet."

So the whale and I set off, as I watched
three furry icebergs moving toward us.

"Here you are," said the whale. I thanked
her and started to run again, but I slipped
on the ice and landed at the feet of three
wise king penguins.

"Help!" I cried, looking over my shoulder at the three polar bears climbing out of the water. The penguins explained that because the wind was blowing north, it would be faster if I ran in that direction.

I ran and ran and ran, straight into a moose.

"Help me, Moose!" I said. "I'm being chased by three polar bears!"

"Let's go!" called the moose. I hopped onto his back and we galloped away. Just as we began to leave the bears in the distance, the moose said, "I know a short cut to get you home."

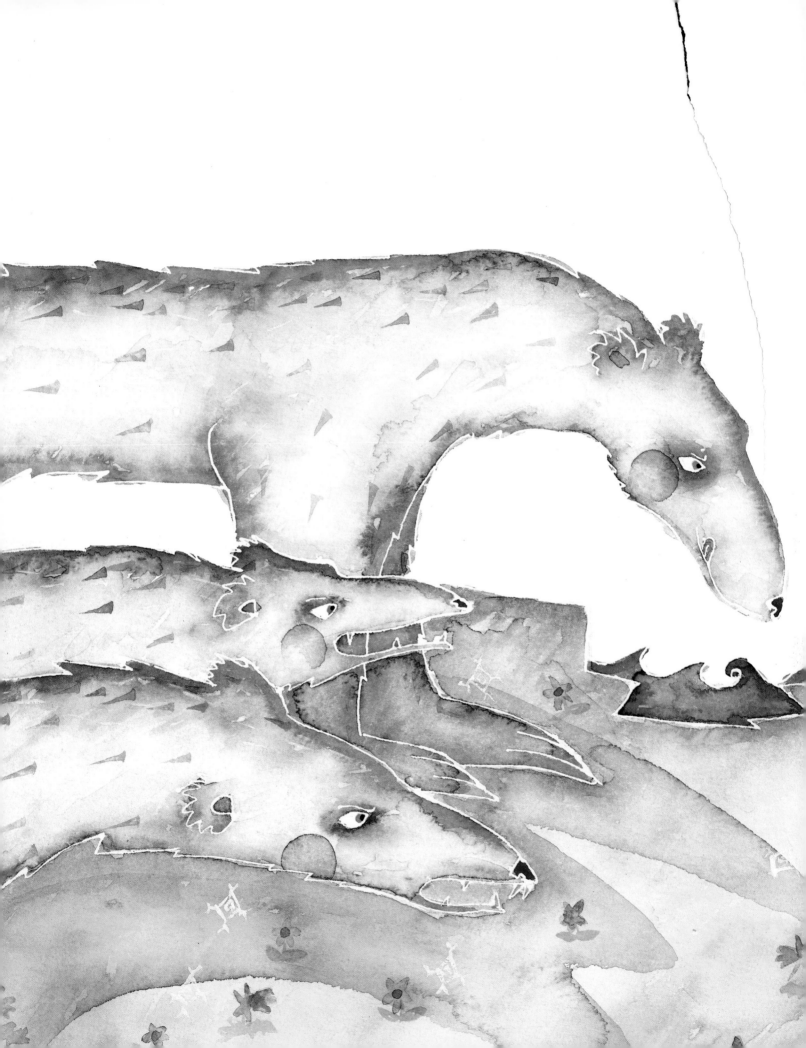

Skidding and sliding across Moose's short cut, I was suddenly thrown through the air and landed bᵘmp! at the feet of the three polar bears, who apparently knew their own short cut.

They gathered around me, and one great white bear lifted his huge paw above my head and said . . .

. . . "Tag! You're it!"

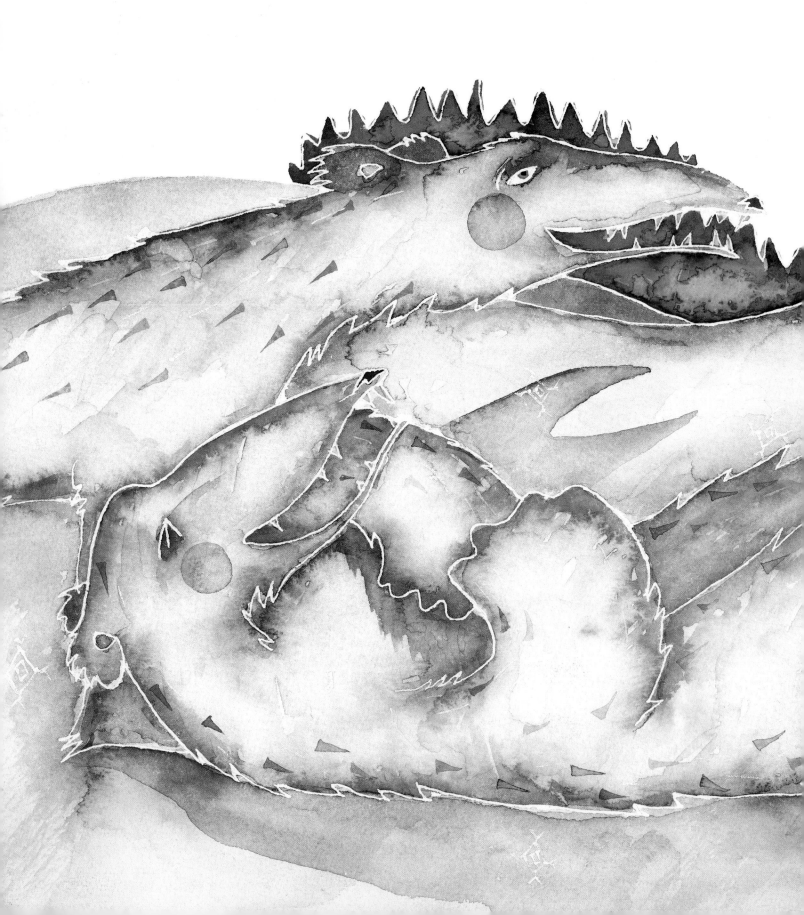